T0162645

THE HOUSE
THAT TALKED

THE HOUSE THAT TALKED

Colin Pitman

authorHOUSE®

AuthorHouse™
1663 Liberty Drive
Bloomington, IN 47403
www.authorhouse.com
Phone: 1-800-839-8640

Published by AuthorHouse   09/07/2012

ISBN: 978-1-4772-2639-1 (sc)
ISBN: 978-1-4772-2638-4 (e)

Cover and illustrations copyright 2012 by Scott Mackay

This book is printed on acid-free paper.

THE HOUSE
THAT TALKED

Scott lived at No:2, Never You Mind Street, Outglassen, Scotland. Scott's house was not unusual, in fact it looked exactly the same as most of the other houses on the street. What was unusual was that the house could talk to Scott and Scott could talk to the house.

Scott lives with his mum, dad and his two older sisters. They were a fairly ordinary type of family. Dad worked, whilst mum stayed home. Scott's sisters had left school but they still lived at home. To his family and everyone else Scott seemed to be just a typical teenager, but inside

No:2 was where Scott's life was very, very different from everyone else.

Scott's adventures and the conversations he had with his house began when Scott and his family moved to Outglassen. Don't ask me why their previous house hadn't talked to Scott, but it hadn't. It may have been that Scott was too young to notice, or he was so busy doing other things that he hadn't time to talk to the walls and furniture in his old house.

Since moving to 'Never You Mind Street' things had begun to change for Scott. To tell you about Scott, his conversations and his adventures with his house, I need to tell you more about the house and the sort of conversations it has with Scott.

The Windows

At No:2, each part of the house, the building, the fixtures and the furniture were like any other house. Of course they all looked different, as they all had a different role and a different part to play. Especially when Scott talked to them and when they talked to Scott. The most important part of the house were the windows. This was because the windows looked out from the house and also looked into every room of the house. The windows, therefore, had a very special position in the house. They always had a lot to say and knew pretty much everything that happened in the house, the garden and the world outside. The windows weren't as knowledgeable about the weather, as the roof. The roof was the expert when it came to what was happening in the skies above Outglassen. So if Scott wanted to get an accurate weather forecast he would always ask the roof.

The Bricks

Although the windows were outnumbered by the bricks of the house, bricks were different. True they covered the whole house, but some of the bricks only faced the outside world. Ask a brick about the world outside or the garden and they could equal whatever the windows had to say. The only problem being, that given the sheer number of bricks in the walls, each one might have a different view. However ask them what was happening in the kitchen just now and they would have no idea at all. You see, they were cut off from what was happening inside by a gap, another set of bricks and then

a coat of plaster. Although the bricks
on the outside were in a good place,
when it came to telling Scott something
interesting, the bricks in the inner wall
were in the worst place of all. These bricks
were constantly in the dark and so they
never talked or heard anything. When the
outside bricks tried to hold a conversation
with them, they never replied. Too much
darkness and the solitude was not good
for them. Over the years it had turned
them mute. They were like the three wise
monkeys, they heard nothing, they saw
nothing and they said nothing. But like
everything that was part of No:2, they
had their role to play and did it well, even
though they were in the dark and it was
very quiet.

The Plaster

Next to the walls is the plaster. Now I am not being negative about plaster but although it was on the inside of the house and in every room, the plaster was, I have to say, a little bit thick. It wasn't thick, thick, as it was only a few centimetres in depth, but it was very dense. This was mainly due to what it was made of. It had no character and despite attempts to liven it up, plaster was plaster.

There is a saying that you can get more sense from talking to a wall. With plaster this was not true. A brick wall yes, you may have got some response, but with a wall that has plaster on it, forget it.

The Curtains

The windows therefore were the heart and soul of the house. They heard most things that happened in and outside the house. They knew what was going on inside every room, even when the curtains or blinds were drawn. How? Well they had developed a good relationship with the curtains. The curtains realised a long time ago that it was in their best interests to talk to the windows. During the night the curtains were the windows ears, during the day they were drawn and folded against the walls. So their ability to hear all that was going on during the day was affected. Anyway if the windows listened very carefully they could hear through the curtains if they wanted, but the windows had to concentrate a lot and they didn't always hear very clearly what the family or the other furniture were talking about. The curtains might cover the windows but they couldn't stop the windows listening in. However unlike bricks and plaster, the windows and curtains were friends and partners and as such they saw it made sense to talk to each other, rather than keep silent.

The Doors

Next were the doors. Two of the doors in the house had very important positions, these were the front and the back doors. Now the front door was also the best looking door. The front door tended to have other fitments put onto it that were very useful. It had a door knocker, which could be a bit of a pain, but thankfully for the front door, the knocker and its accompanying strike plate was far better for the door than being hit all over with a set of boney knuckles. The letter flap was also useful, it could be a bit lippy at times and in the wind it struggled to keep its flap shut, but nevertheless, when the postman arrived it had the opportunity to scan the mail and let the door know if there was anything of interest. Most of it might be junk mail, but occasionally there were some very interesting items of post passing through the letter flap and when it saw something of interest it just had to tell the door all the latest gossip.

Anyway the front door was always on guard and was usually the first part of the house to get a really good look at whoever was visiting or staying at the house. The windows might see who was coming before the door, but the door was the one that got a really good close up of any visitors.

The back door was the more functional and workmanlike of the two doors. It very rarely had anybody new to talk about and unlike the front door he was often left open, and as we all know when is a door not a door, when it is ajar. The back door saw most of the comings and goings of the family and any trades people who visited, but it was very clear in the hierarchy of doors that the front door was the top dog.

Throughout the rest of the house there were lots of other doors but they were not as important as the front and back door. You see they only led from one room to the next. When they were being opened and closed they could shout to each other but most of the time they kept the secrets of the rooms to themselves. Anyway it was no good talking to the plaster wall opposite. The plaster just looked at them with a blank expression on its face and said nothing.

The toilet door had the worst job. Whenever it tried to talk to the landing or the hallway, they would turn their noses up and pretend not to listen. Being a toilet door was not the best. Apart from its role in the house, of keeping what happens in the toilet quiet, it also had to contend with being slammed quite a bit. If any door was going to be slammed then it tended to be the one leading to the loo. Even Scott didn't mean to shut it so fiercely at times, it just seemed to slam. The hallway and the landing didn't like the toilet, and this also meant that they didn't particularly like the door to the toilet being left open. So they encouraged draughts in the house to make sure the toilet door stayed shut. This meant on occasions that for no apparent reason the door to the toilet would suddenly slam shut. Sometimes the toilet door slammed itself, particularly if it was embarrassed by either the smells from the toilet or some of the conversations between the toilet and the loo brush.

The Toilet

Next I suppose I ought to talk about the toilet itself. Vital I know in any house but really it did have the worst place and job. You see unlike other parts or fixtures in the house, the toilet was a one trick pony. People only went to the toilet for one thing. The need and the calls of nature to the occupants of No 2. Although the toilets were tastefully decorated and perfumed, for most of the time it had one of the worst jobs in the house. The loo didn't get involved in the hustle and bustle of the house, nor did it join in any of the fun and games that took place. So the loo, either with its lid up and able to speak, or lid down and it was silent, was not the nicest part of the house. The loo had to deal with the occupants of the house for the shortest of times and when they had to go to the loo, what happened in there was not pleasant.

When Scott went to the loo it only had a very brief time to try and talk to him. So when the toilet heard the door open and saw Scott he only had a brief moment to try and speak. It therefore tried to make whatever it wanted to try and say either funny or outrageous, but then it would all go wrong due to the very difficult circumstances of their conversation. You see Scott was always in a hurry and only wanted to see the toilet at critical times. When Scott had the time to sit for any length of time he was always wondering what the toilet was mumbling about. The loo tried to hold conversations with Scott about, for example, the state of the nation or the latest discovery that had been made down at the sewage works, but Scott couldn't hear very clearly. The toilet was always struggling to get itself heard as it was either dealing with what Scott had eaten the day before or having difficulty in making what it said heard. This was the biggest problem, as anything the toilet said when Scott was sat on the loo was always aimed at the wrong part of Scott's anatomy.

If Scott did rush out and leave the toilet seat up and the toilet had the freedom to talk, then its friends in the loo were not very receptive. All the other parts of the toilet area were just as boring as the toilet. As they too had a mundane job to do. When they did deign to talk to each other their conversations were at best described as lavatorial, at their worst, talking dirty. They couldn't help themselves just when they started to hold a reasonable conversation the loo brush would spoil it with a smutty one liner or the toilet seat would tell a bottom joke. No one could hear their laughter, only the toilet door and whenever he tried to tell the rest of the house via the hallway he would be silenced very quickly and noisily. Hence that's why the toilet door tended to be slammed shut.

The Kitchen

Now where do we go next, the kitchen? Well the kitchen thought itself the most important room in the house. The kitchen used to be small, shabby looking and very functional, a bit like the toilet but with much better hygiene and with definitely better things to talk about. However the kitchens in all houses were recently getting a bit of a make over and as No2 was a new house it was fitted out with all the latest gadgets and appliances. The kitchen no longer had boring Belfast sinks that were forever moaning about how bad it all was especially when it had all the dirty dishes and pans to contend with.

Strange isn't it, that some of the old sinks were either destined to become nothing more than a trough for plants and left out in the rain, or they would reappear as chic white sinks in the new very glamorous modern fitted kitchens. Even though conditions had changed for all sinks, with the dishwasher taking over the washing of the pots, you only have to give a sink a few breakfast or dinner dishes to contend with and they soon revert back to their old ways. Moan Moan Moan.

Now the kitchen at No:2 Never You Mind Street was the heart and soul of the house. Full of technology, gadgets and it was very upmarket. Of all the rooms in the house this was the most cosmopolitan and also the noisiest for Scott. You see the kitchen had appliances from all over the world and the rivalry and the attempts at one one-upmanship was something to wonder at. For a start Scott couldn't understand all the languages being spoken. The German dishwasher was constantly having a battle with the Italian washing machine. They both stood side by side either side of the sink and to listen to battles about their efficiency and environmental credentials in German and Italian did Scott's head in.

When the Japanese microwave was switched on, what it could say about the food it could cook and the time it took, would have made the English cooker's oven overheat with anger. Well it should have, that is if the oven had been able to speak Japanese. With all this noise and the competition that went on in the kitchen Scott didn't stay in the kitchen any longer than necessary. He did have one friend in the kitchen one that he could understand and talk to and that was their very large and very imposing American Fridge. Or Billy the Fridge or Bad Fat as Scott called him. Scott gave him the nickname Bad Fat, as his mum would always say that when Scott sneaked something from his fridge friend it was bad for him, and Fat as the fridge always seemed to be full to overflowing. Bad Fat, Billy the Fridge was also the most interesting appliance in the kitchen as he would take on all the stories and tales that he learnt from his collection of fridge magnets that seemed to cover his body. He also had loads of very interesting tales about how he arrived in Scotland and all his adventures when he was in the kitchen appliance warehouse in Outglassen. Bad fat was also well liked by everyone in the house. So much so that when they had a really good holiday, they would bring back something of interest to stick to his sides. So with all these mementoes of holidays they had enjoyed stuck to his side he always had something interesting to tell Scott. Being a fridge, he also heard the tales from the food that mum would constantly be putting on his shelves. Billy would also listen in to the late night conversations round the kitchen table that the adults would have. If Scott had time in the morning he would tell him all the little bits of gossip or anything he thought Scott would want to know. Scott, if he could, would have spent hours with the door wide open listening to the fridge, but for Bad Fat Billy, this was not good for his health. Too much talking to Scott, however interesting, was definitely not good. Too much chattering with the door open meant Billy the Fridge would

overheat and as we all know, a warm
fridge is no good to anyone

Having now introduced a few of the
rooms, furniture and characters that
made up the house, it's probably best if
I now tell you some of the stories and
the goings on in the house. Along the
way there will be plenty more characters
who will have their say. Including the
cupboard under the stairs. This was a
dark and mysterious place and as all
children and Scott knew only too well, one
of the scariest places in a house. I'll tell
you about the cupboard under the stairs
later. Much later

Dad's Not Well

Scott was walking up the path on his way back from school, as he looked up at No:2 the windows all winked at him and as he got closer they clearly had something to say. As he walked up to the house the path had very little to say other than moan about the cat from the house opposite. The cat had had the cheek to wander over to Number 2 and sun itself on the path outside the house. The path was not happy. Paths like to be clear of all obstructions as they like to provide a clear access and exit for the house. They do not like bikes, clothing and especially cats lying along their uncluttered lines.

Despite all the paths attempts to talk to Scott he wasn't interested in what the cat had been doing, whilst lazing around in the sun, he could sense, as soon as he started to walk up the path that the windows were eager to tell him something.

"Scott" the windows all shouted in chorus, "Your Dads not well. Mum's in a tizz, Doctor's been and the whole house is in uproar. And if I was you I'd keep away from the sofa". Scott didn't have time to hear any more as he was now at the front door and as he opened the door, it spoke to him.

"Scott the doctors been, I think your dad must be quite poorly. He didn't go out to work this morning and he seems to have spent most of the day in the lounge. We are all very concerned, well apart from the sofa. If anybody special arrives, I will let you know" The door was very precise and gave his message to Scott very much like a butler might have. If Scott's family could have afforded a butler.

"Thanks door but you are a bit late as I have already had an early warning from the windows" Scott replied. The door did its best to not look upset but inside it was seething. "Windows" it mumbled to itself. "Always shouting and getting in first. Gives the house a bad name on the street. So common. Why can't they wait and let the door do its job" The door was clearly not happy and decided that it would close with a slam and make the windows rattle. This was nothing to do with Scott. The door was obviously upset that he should have been the first to tell Scott. He was the front door after all. Windows, he thought, open or shut they couldn't keep their mouths closed for one second. Fancy shouting down the path at Scott like that. If he had his way they would be boarded up on a permanent basis.

Scott stood in the hallway. "Scott is that you?" Mum called from the kitchen, having heard the door close. Scott didn't answer he just slunk into the lounge.

Everything was quiet and slightly darker than normal. The curtains were closed and they seemed to be sleeping in fact the whole room seemed to be standing still and holding it's breath.

The Sofa's not happy

"Scott" a hushed voice came from the direction of the sofa. "Scott, he's over here. It's your dad and he's wrapped up in the quilt that he's draped over me"

"He's been here most of the day. Any chance you could get him to go to bed. Best place for him I think, given his condition. It wouldn't be so bad but he's been sweating on and off and he can't keep still. Don't mind the moving about but this dampness is not attractive. Hope he doesn't leave an odour. The annoying thing is that he's also brought down that massive king size quilt to lie under and as it's a Monday I normally have an afternoon watching the day time programmes. 'Visit the Country' is on and it's my favourite programme on a Monday. I can't see a thing. The quilts been watching on and off and won't tell me anything, he's so wrapped up in your dad and my programme. It's not fair, your dad should be at work" The sofa was clearly upset.

"What!" Scott said. "What's got into you. Dad's not well and all you are concerned about is your personal hygiene problems and a chance to sit and watch day time TV. You are so selfish".

"Scott, you don't understand I am not set up to be a hospital bed. I'm a sofa" The sofa replied.

Scott turned half expecting the other furniture to have their say, but they all went quiet as his mum had just come into the room.

"Scott, why didn't you reply when I called" she asked.

"Sorry mum but I saw the curtains were closed and so I just came straight into the lounge. How's dad?" Scott replied.

"Not too good Scott best come into the kitchen and I'll tell you what's been happening" With that they both left the lounge. Scott and mum walked through the hallway on their way to the kitchen. As he passed the hall mirror Scott heard it say something but didn't quite catch everything it had to say. Well no doubt he would pick up on the mirror's reflections on what had been happening during the day.

Later

Mum explains

When they got into the kitchen mum started to tell Scott all about what had been going on.

"Scott your Dad hasn't been well since this morning, quite poorly and so I called the doctor. He's had a look at him and he thinks it might be food poisoning, not sure how but looks like he's going to be off work for a couple of days at least. We need to be quiet and not make too much noise to let dad get some sleep"

"Mum shouldn't dad be in bed then" Scott was enquiring through his own concern for dad and nothing to do with the sofa's representations. There was a bit of his own agenda as well, as having a sick dad downstairs might restrict Scott from playing on his game machine.

"I have suggested that he goes upstairs to bed, but all I got was a shrug and a low groan. So I've decided to leave him where he is for the time being. Perhaps in a bit I could try and persuade him to have an early night, we'll see" Mum said

Having got the low down from mum Scott decided to get changed out of his school things and also check out the rest of the house.

"Going upstairs mum to change, what's for tea"

"Thought we would have cheese on toast, OK?" Mum shouted after Scott as he left the kitchen.

"Fine" Scott headed for the stairs. On his way he decided to check out the mirror.

How's yersel

"Hi you" Scott said, as he stopped to look in the mirror. The mirror looked back "Hi you, how's yersel" It replied.

The mirror had been bought in Glasgow and still retained some of the Glaswegian patter. This mirror, like all mirrors, had attitude. Something, I think, with the need to be reflective. Also mirrors are all very different. Have you ever noticed that in some mirrors you look better than in others. This is not just about how they are made but the fact that no two mirrors are the same due to the attitude that mirrors adopt during their life looking out from their place on the wall. You see, if you offend a mirror they then do their utmost to put you in a bad light. Be nice to a mirror and they make you look good. Only trouble is, once you have offended a mirror, no matter how hard you try you won't change it's view about you. This mirror liked Scott and Scott liked what he saw. But the mirror due to its Glaswegian heritage also had an extra edge to its attitude.

"Lookin guid Scott, which is more than I can say for your da, by the way. He looked terrible when he was here this morning. I kent something was wrong. First thing he did was stick his tongue out at me. Well on reflection he did it to himsel, but we mirrors can be offended you know. It's amazing some of the sights I see. The mirror was keen to give Scott all the information from this mornings observations.

"And as you know Scott when you look into the mirror, all I can see, you can see. I also got a brief glimpse of yer mam and the doctor earlier. She looked concerned, the doctor less so. He seemed to have other things on his mind other than your da. So how is the old man by the way, haven't seen him for awhile" The mirror added.

"Not sure the last time I saw him he was covered from head to toe in a quilt and all I got was the sofa giving me grief about missing his programmes on TV" Scott looked deep into the mirror almost expecting to see another face beside his.

"Och he's a lazy so and so that sofa, has his feet down all day and nothing to do till night time. Then all he does is make people uncomfortable so they might sit elsewhere and he can catch up on his soaps and the movies. Only time you can get a good cosy on that sofa is when he nods off from too much telly his sel. You might also want to check oot the lavvie. When I did catch a wee glimpse of your da that was where he was heading, and he seemed to be in a bit of a hurry. I had hoped that the hall would have got an update from the lavvie, but you know that

the hall is nae friendly wi the lavvie door.
That lot have never got on, something
to do with all the less than savoury
conversations that's passed between them
over the years. Not to mention some of
the odours that the hallway has had to put
up with" The mirror was giving Scott the
low down on all of today's comings and
goings in the hall.

"Fine I'll go in and have a bit of a chat
later, only I don't need to go just yet. Not
that I have a lot to say to the loo whenever
I go in there anyway" Scott replied

With that Scott left from the mirror and
headed towards the stairs.

The Stairs

Now stairs are a bit strange. You see stairs in general are always in a bit of a dither. When they are put into a house they know in what direction they should go. Up. However after they have had a few people going up and down they get a bit confused. I suppose it is bound to happen as people go up and then use the same stairs to come down. Stairs therefore try and have a code to themselves if they feel a toe, the person is going up and if they feel a heel then the person is going down. Unfortunately this is not always the case and so you have situations where people using the stairs slip as the step is confused between a toe appearing to be going up and someone's heel appearing to be someone going down. Confusing isn't it. Also sometimes the stair is at fault as it confuses the person using the stairs. Most times people go up stairs with a clear decision to go up. However halfway up they remember something and so they stop to try and decide whether they should continue up or down. This is partly the stairs fault and partly their own. For this reason stairs can also be quite dangerous places to have changes of mind. You only need to make a going up or a coming down mistake or go too fast so the stairs doesn't have time to get ready for which way you are going and then there's trouble. Usually the floor in the hall gets the brunt of the disagreement between stairs and your body but the individual also has a few bumps and bruises to show for the mix up on the stairs. So always remember be careful on the stairs. Stairs are ditherers and you are the one who will suffer the most from their indecisions.

Stairs are also not reliable sources of information. You see it all has to do with the number of steps between top and bottom, or the bottom and the top. The message at either end might start off very clear but as it goes through each step then like Chinese whispers the message gets changed or distorted. How do I know? Well the next time somebody goes upstairs and you shout a message, see how many times the person replies. "You what?". Now if they had been in a straight line and the same distance apart and with no stairs in between then they would have heard your call very clearly. But put a set of steps in between and with all the steps wanting to pass on the message then it all gets mixed up and confused!

Anyway Scott decided to go upstairs. He hadn't time to sit on the bottom step and chat. Not sure if that would be any help anyway. Talking to one step at the top or the bottom of a stairs is best if you want a straight forward chat, as the step is talking on a one to one basis and you clearly are either at the top or the bottom of the stairs. That is why I think they make naughty children sit on the bottom of the stairs when parents want them to think about their behaviour. Parents wouldn't want to risk them learning a lesson halfway up the stairs as the message would get confused. Equally people will often sit at the top of stairs, when they are thinking about doing something downstairs. Helps have a clear mind with no other steps in the way. It is my view that very few good decisions are made either part way up or down stairs.

In bed

So Scott ran up stairs to go to his
bedroom. At least in there, he thought, he
would have some peace and quiet and not
be bothered by the house and the news
that Dad was not well. He hadn't been
home long and all the conversations he
had had with mum or the house had all
been about Dad. He wasn't being selfish
but he had news about school and his
friends and what the teacher had said to
him and loads, loads more to talk about,
but Dad being at home seemed to be the
most important information of the day.

The upstairs landing tried to say something to him but Scott was too quick and he soon reached the safety of his room. As the window was about to say something Scott quickly drew the curtains. He knew that any message would not get through as his bright animal print lined curtains that were put up in Scott's bedroom had an arrangement with Scott. Scott had an agreement with his bedroom curtain. Scott would only talk to his bedroom curtains if they didn't say anything to the windows. Scott made this deal with the curtains to give himself that bit more privacy in his bedroom.

But as Scott lay on his bed, the bed was the first to speak. "Hey Scott what are you doing here at this time of day. Not ill are you?" Scott didn't reply.

Obviously the bed had thankfully been asleep since being made this morning and so had not heard anything about Dad and his illness. Brilliant, Scott thought, I now have time to myself with no more, "Your Dads not well". As Scott lay back on his pillow, the pillow asked him why he was on his bed at this time. Pillows are special they are the holders of your dreams, they store all your absent thoughts when you are trying to get to sleep and then replay them back in all different ways. Dream makers. Pillows can be temperamental though, sometimes when Scott goes to bed and his pillow isn't ready to replay his thoughts as dreams Scott struggles to sleep. The pillow feels so uncomfortable as it tries to sort itself out. Some nights when the pillow has got its game together as soon as Scott's head touches the pillow it so soft, comfortable and receptive that he goes straight to sleep and into his dreams. Today however, as he lay there, it was clear to the pillow that Scott wasn't going to go to sleep, so he made himself as uncomfortable as possible. Scott couldn't rest his head on the pillow so he decided to go back downstairs. He thought he'd have a chat with Billy the Fridge before tea.

As he got up from his bed he was a little bit annoyed that both the bed and the pillow were relieved to see him leave. They did say sorry and promised that on his return he would have a good nights sleep. Something Scott was looking forward too. As he got to the top of stairs he thought he ought to have a word with the stairs. Given all that had been happening he didn't want any upsets as he went down. "Now stairs I'm going down, so don't give me any hassle"

Scott made the hallway without any problems but was a bit taken back to hear the bottom step ask "Hey Scott what's this about you wearing a crown, the one with the tassel".

"Stairs" Scott said. "Don't trust them. They always get the message wrong"

Billy the Fridge

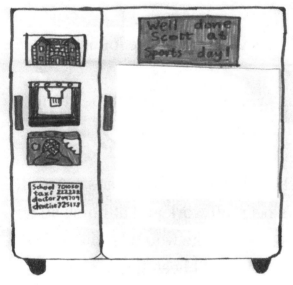

Bad Fat was stood by the kitchen door as usual. Mum was busy with dad in the lounge so he decided it would be a good time to have a chat. Opening the door Bad Fat welcomed him with a "Hi buddy.

School over and do you want a snack before dinner? I've got lots on offer. Your mum's not about is she?" Bad Fat Billy was feeling pretty generous today.

"Nah" Scott replied.

"Mum's with dad in the lounge".

"Hey, what's dad doing home at this time"? The fridge asked.

"I thought you'd heard, dads not well. He's been off work and at home all day". Scott thought he would let the fridge know what had been happening.

"Dude what's up with him, he seemed all right last night"

"Food poisoning, according to mum, I haven't had chance to chat to him yet, as he is wrapped up in a quilt in the lounge" Scott stood looking longingly into the cold cavern of a fridge.

"Whoa you don't think it was that French cheese he snacked on last night. Only he started the night with a few beers and I could see he was a man on a mission. He had that look in his eye. I'm sure he would have been OK with most of the stuff that he was mauling, but then he moved the low calorie yoghurts and his eyes lit up when he saw the cheese. Now I have tried to tell your mum about that mouldy French dairy product, but where she is normally so good with the stuff she buys, if you want my opinion, mouldy old cheese can't be trusted. The darn thing came in here with mould already on its back. I know that some of these cheese guys are made that way but whereas your true blue British Stilton guy tends to behave itself, with the Italian and French stuff you just need to keep an eye on em. Not an expert on the stuff but I knew that French number was bad news. He hadn't been here five minutes and my shelves were giving me the warning signs. Anyway all this talk of that mouldy stuff and the info about your dad being under the weather, it's got me all warmed up. I'm getting a bit hot under the collar, which as you know Scott ain't no good for me. Man its been good to talk to you but I need to chill out for a bit. Know what I mean. Just close the door and get back to me when you can" The fridge sounded a bit worried so Scott slowly closed Billy's huge door.

Scott had wanted to talk some more but he realised that to do so would not have been good for Bad Fat. So he had reluctantly closed the door, but he was now much wiser about how dad might not be well. Billy's tip off about the mouldy cheese might be helpful. Trouble was how could he tell mum as he didn't want to give away his conversation with Billy the Fridge.

Scott had in the past tried to tell mum about his conversations with the house when all the talking had first started, but mum either seemed too busy or she just gave him a, well that's interesting kind of look, and went on with her daily chores around the house. After several attempts he just didn't bother any more. No he would tell her he'd noticed that the funny smell in the fridge had gone away and was

that anything to do with dad's illness. Dad had probably said something anyway.
Just as he was about to settle down with his laptop and have a chat with his state of the art computer, his mum came in the kitchen.

"Scott you haven't been in the fridge and snacking have you" mum asked

"No I was just looking mum. Mum have you noticed that that funny smell in the fridge has disappeared? Only I was looking to grab a yoghurt to eat, but for the past couple of days I haven't quite fancied them as it seemed to be a bit whiffy in that area." Scott tried to sound as convincing as possible.

"What, you think the yoghurts might be off. I hope not they were only bought the other day." Mum went over to the fridge to have a look for herself.

Billy was still working hard to get down to temperature as Scott could hear his motor whirring away in the background. Bad Fat Billy wouldn't be pleased, but he knew he wouldn't say anything to mum.

"Scott have you moved anything or thrown anything away when you were in the fridge?" Mum was looking quizzically at the shelves where the yoghurts where.

"No mum, just looking, I haven't taken anything out, why?" Scott replied.

"Nothing just that there is a bit more space on the shelf where the yoghurt's where." Mum said no more, but shut the fridge and left the room.

Before she left she called back to Scott.

"Scott wash your hands I'm going to get dinner in five minutes."

The toilet has its say

Scott decided to go to the downstairs loo. As he closed the door he knew it was probably a mistake. The seat was up and he knew the toilet just couldn't wait to start up a conversation with him.

"Look loo before you say anything. I know my dads not well and I am sure he has been in here a couple of times today." Scott thought he would get in the first word, as he knew the loo and his cronies would be quick to report on anything out of the unusual. Dad being at home and probably using the loo would be major news to this lot.

"Scott you've spoilt our day." the loo, the brush, the sink and the mirror all screamed in unison.

"Sorry guys but I have heard nothing else since I got in from school. I am sure you all understand that before I get to you I have to pass through a number of rooms and doors. Dad not being well and off work is all I've heard since walking up the garden path". Scott thought he'd let them know that there wasn't much more to say about Dad, but he was wrong.

"Well you will be amazed at what we've got to tell you" The loo made his play to attract Scott's attention, and it worked.

"What?" Although Scott had initially come into the toilet to wash his hands he had also thought about spending a penny.

It had been a long journey from school
to home after all. The loo's comments
stopped Scott in his tracks.

"News loo, what news could you possibly
have that I haven't heard already?" Scott
sounded surprised

"Well Scott you're not the only one who
can have conversations with the house,
your dad has the gift as well"

Scott was amazed. "Dad has been talking
to you"?

"Yep" said the loo. "Been in here a couple
of times today. We have had a number
of conversations. He has been telling me
how ill he has been and that it's not going
to happen ever again. Told me he knew
he shouldn't have eaten the cheese and

although he didn't look too well he was so eager to talk to me. So eager in fact that he got down on his hands and knees to speak directly to me. I think his illness has triggered off his ability to talk to us" The loo was positively beaming with his new revelation, if toilets can beam that is. Scott wondered if the loo had probably misread what had been happening. After all they did lead a very sheltered life in this room. Dad had put some reading material in, but that hadn't been for their benefit.

"Loo I think this is a bit of wishful thinking on your part. Dad on his knees and talking to you is something people do when they are ill. Dad was probably reflecting on his mistake in eating some mouldy cheese last night rather than

holding a conversation with you." Scott
was trying to let the toilet down gently

"What, no I am sure you are wrong Scott.
I know he had an upset tummy and all
that but he's never spoken to me like that
before. It was a real heart to heart sort
of thing. He spent a good deal of time in
here. I am sure he has the ability Scott"
The toilet did sound convincing.

At this point the mirror also joined in.
"Scott your dad has been talking to me as
well. He looked so closely at me and he
was really concentrating on what he was
saying to me. Told me all about the cheese
and that he's not going to eat anything
that comes from France ever again". The
mirror said confidently.

Scott couldn't believe his ears, dad in conversation with the house. He had to find out if this was true.

"Wait here I am going to check this out. I'll be back." Scott rushed out the toilet. He hadn't had time to wash his hands and he had also completely forgot to spend a penny. If true this was really important and everything else could wait.

As he entered the hallway, mum was just going into the kitchen.

"Scott, dinner is in five minutes and your dads feeling better. He won't be having anything to eat just yet but at least he's back in the land of the living" Mum passed Scott on her way to the kitchen

"Mum is it OK to say hello to dad?"

"Yes but don't get too close, I think I know what caused his illness but best be sure that its not a bug or something. Don't be long just say hello" As Mum disappeared into the kitchen

Scott hurried to the lounge.

Dad explains

Scott poked his head round the door. The quilt that had just been a mound, but now it had a distinct head to it. The previous mound of bedding that Scott had seen before looked now like a very large albino turtle.

"Hi Dad, how are you?" Scott enquired.

"Aw Scott, good to see you. Not been too well. It's been a terrible day." Dad didn't move his head much more out of the quilt, as he was still feeling a bit queasy.

"Dad sorry you aren't feeling too well, but would you mind if I asked you something?" Scott thought he would cut to the chase, as Dad sounded under the weather.

"Yeh fine what is it" the albino turtle replied.

"Dad have you been talking to the toilet?" Scott decided to be forthright.

"What, what? If you mean have I, as some people might say been talking to the porcelain, then yes. As your Mum has probably told you I have been to the toilet to be sick several times today and talking away to myself, but that was just me rambling on about how ill I felt. What's with you asking me if I have been talking to the toilet. I haven't left a mess in there have I. If so I really am sorry. I was careful but then I haven't been well". Dad explained.

Scott didn't need to hear any more he'd got the message loud and clear, Dads conversation was nothing to do with being able to talk to the toilet or the mirror or any of the fixture or fittings in the downstairs loo. This was dad being very, very ill and as Scott sometimes did when he was in the toilet he talked to himself. Dad didn't and hadn't been having a conversation with the toilet, he'd just been talking out loud.

"Oh nothing dad, everything's fine. Hope you get better." With that he left the lounge

He strode across the hall, he opened
the toilet door and shouted to a wide
mouthed toilet, an expectant mirror and a
very attentive toilet brush.

"Morons, your all morons, the lot of you"
Scott shouted.

Scott didn't wait for a reply, he closed the
door with a slam and went straight into
the kitchen and sat down to have his tea.
He was now about to eat beans on toast
and not his usual cheese on toast.

It was clear that mum was not taking any
more chances with dodgy dairy products,
well not today any way.

"Scott, what did you shout just now?"
Mum was stood at the cooker with the

noise of the extractor whirring away above her.

"Nothing Mum, must have been the telly". Scott thought he wouldn't say anything to Mum. There was no point. For the time being, Scott was the only one who could have a conversation with the house, despite what the loo and the rest of the cronies in the downstairs toilet might think.

In the toilet it was all very quiet. None of them wanted to say anything. They were too embarrassed.

This story is just one of the many adventures that Scott had with the House that Talked. There will be others.